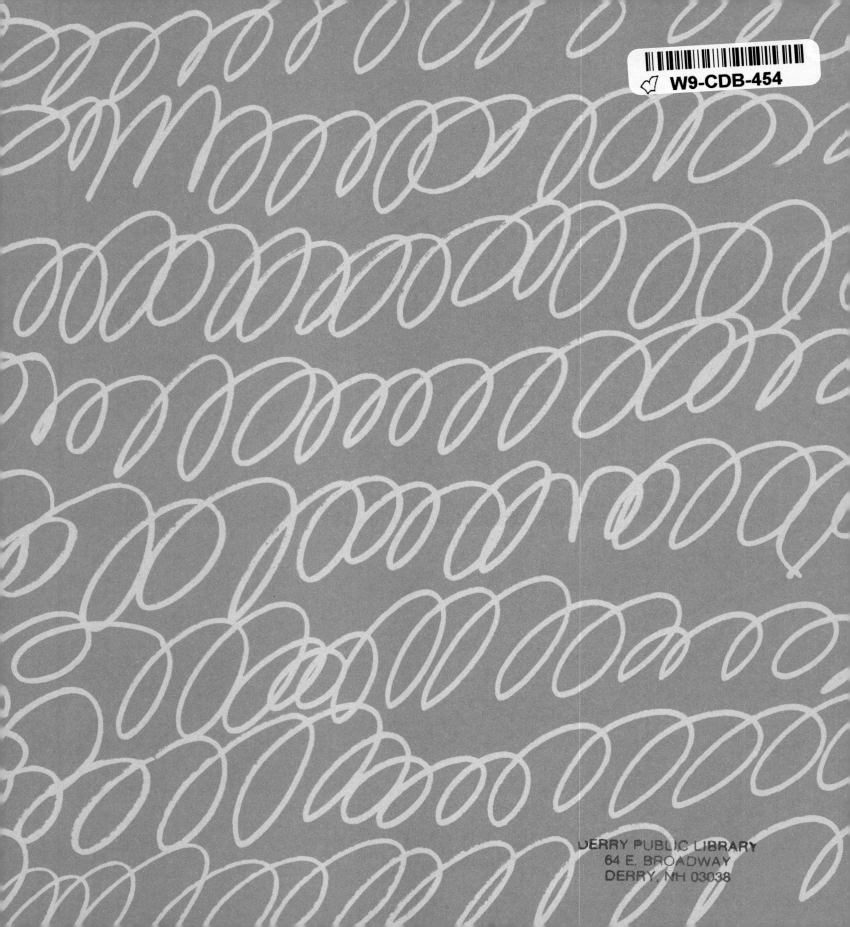

A SQUIGGLY STORY

To Yvette, For helping turn my squiggles into stories — A.L.

To Mom and Dad, who raised me to love books and music and making things.
And Katrin and Allister, who make my life pretty awesome. — M.L.

Kids Can Press acknowledges the financial support of the Government of Ontario, through the Ontario Media Development Corporation's Ontario Book Initiative; the Ontario Arts Council; the Canada Council for the Arts; and the Government of Canada, through the CBF, for our publishing activity.

Published in Canada by
Kids Can Press Ltd.
25 Dockside Drive
Toronto, ON M5A 0B5

Published in the U.S. by
Kids Can Press Ltd.
2250 Military Road
Tonawanda, NY 14150

www.kidscanpress.com

The artwork in this book was rendered in Photoshop.
The text is set in Italo Light and Haneda Semi Bold.

Edited by Yvette Ghione
Designed by Karen Powers

This book is smyth sewn casebound.
Manufactured in Malaysia in 6/2016, by Tien Wah Press (Pte) Ltd.

CM 16   0 9 8 7 6 5 4 3 2

LIBRARY AND ARCHIVES CANADA CATALOGUING IN PUBLICATION

Larsen, Andrew, 1960-, author
       A squiggly story / written by Andrew Larsen ;
illustrated by Mike Lowery.

ISBN 978-1-77138-016-4 (bound)

       I. Lowery, Mike, 1980-, illustrator II. Title.

PS8623.A77S68 2016   jC813'.6   C2015-907086-4

Kids Can Press is a Corus Entertainment Inc. company

A SQUIGGLY STORY

Written by
ANDREW LARSEN

Illustrated by
MIKE LOWERY

KIDS CAN PRESS

SOMETIMES I PRETEND
I CAN WRITE, TOO.

BIG LETTERS AND LITTLE LETTERS.

SWIRL AFTER SWIRL.
SQUIGGLE AFTER SQUIGGLE.

SO I GET MY CRAYONS AND PENCILS AND
A PAD OF PAPER AND I START TO WRITE.
I START WITH A SINGLE LETTER.

IT'S AN **EASY** LETTER.

SO I DO A BUNCH OF DOTS
FOR THE SAND ON THE BEACH · · · ·

THEN I MAKE A BUNCH OF V's.

BIG V's AND (LITTLE) v's.

WAVE AFTER WAVE IN THE OCEAN.

"YOU HAVE A BEGINNING. NOW WE'RE IN THE MIDDLE OF THE STORY. SOMETHING ELSE HAS TO HAPPEN SO WE CAN GET TO THE END."

I'M STUCK AGAIN.

I START DOODLING.

I DOODLE ANOTHER **V**.

BUT THIS TIME I DOODLE IT
UPSIDE DOWN.

IT'S GETTING CLOSER AND CLOSER!

I FLIP THE PAGE TO GET AWAY FROM THE SHARK.

Once upon a time there was a brother and a sister and they loved to play soccer.

One day they had an idea. They decided to play soccer on the beach. So they went to the beach and played soccer.

ALIA OFFERS ANOTHER IDEA.
What if the shark's name is SQUIGGLES?
What if SQUIGGLES is a VAMPIRE shark?
What if she invites the brother and sister to ride on her back?
And what if they become a VAMPIRE FAMILY and live forever?
VAMPIRES CAN'T SWIM.
Everyone knows that.
Of course they can swim.
VAMPIRES can do ANYTHING.

SO, I GET MY PENCIL AND I START WITH A BUNCH OF STARS.

THEN I ADD A FEW EXCLAMATION MARKS. MY SISTER TOLD ME EXCLAMATION MARKS MAKE THINGS EXCITING. SHE'S RIGHT! IT IS EXCITING!

I ADD A COUPLE OF SLANTY LINES.

"WHAT'S GOING ON?" ASKS MY SISTER, LOOKING UP FROM HER BOOK.

It's nighttime. The stars are out. The shark has gone away and we decide to take a walk on the beach. That's when we discover this GIANT ROCKET SHIP.

That sounds cool. Then what happens?

"NOT YET!" I SAY, ADDING ONE MORE SQUIGGLE. "JUST BEFORE THE ROCKET BLASTS OFF WE SPY A **MARTIAN** LOOKING OUT THROUGH A WINDOW. THE MARTIAN INVITES US TO CLIMB ABOARD."

That's a GREAT ending!

NOW I HAVE AN IDEA FOR MY **NEXT** STORY. IT'S GOING TO BE ABOUT A BOY WHO CLIMBS ABOARD A ROCKET SHIP AND TAKES A **TRIP TO MARS.**

AND I THINK I KNOW JUST **HOW** TO BEGIN.